I have loved; not sexually I have reserved that for Myself.

Table of Contents

Last Night I Dreamed

Last night
I dreamed most vivid
I laid against your chest
as you caressed and loved me until
my body flamed from unrest

I cried
silently because my
dream was not reality

Last night
I dreamed the unimaginable

I thought about you as I lied awake wiping
my tears that only I could see and my heart
could feel

Ripe

It's so ripe
the juice oozes out
and runs down my legs
wouldn't you like for the nectar
to run down the sides of your mouth
the probing of your strong hands as
you grasp the pit of my fruit makes
me squirm
put your hand in
oh! a little deeper up way past my
ahh! you have the pit now kiss my lips
so that I can taste the sweetness, too!

Jelly and Wetness

If the flesh is weak then mine is jelly
a bitch in heat creaming and screaming
longing for release.
Every bitter thing taste sweet to me,
the sights are new the smells are fresh.

If love were to find me, I'd sure be obliged
if he would possess the fire of you; who kissed me
yesterday, setting my soul aflame and leaving me
to dwell upon your kiss.

While every man was quickly forgotten even
the man whom I share a bed.
Time seemed to stall, while I nestled in your embrace.

LOVE

Make love to me
while the heat of you
consumes my
body
I will
make love to you
tracing the lines of your
masculinity
with my tongue
the
love you have shown me
is more than I have hoped for
and
I just want to LOVE you in return

Traveling the World

Against the porcelain tile
feeling the warmth
of the water
I press the soap against
my vagina
and apply pressure
where shall I take myself today
the bath (ROME)
the living room (PARIS)
the kitchen (ITALY)
the bedroom (AFRICA)
the hallway (the CANALS of VENICE)

Sexual Reflection 1

I believe the men I have experienced
think that as a woman,
I have learned sex through my body.
I believe it is what SEX is in
my Mind.

Sexual Reflections 2

Let the coolness in my room
dry me off naturally
from lip to lip
I touch me
I taste me

Two People in Love

The half opened window
invites the cool wind
the oak tree casts a shadow
of itself against the wall the leaves depict
a mural of an alluring dance
it was a saltation so sensuous
a sight to have seen
they were gyrating so easy
yet slow
the dance of two people
two people in love
night has passed swiftly
the mural is gone
time that has lapsed is now
a new day has begun
the cool wind has been constant
the oak tree is calm
the leaves that imaged a dance
so alluring is done
all that is left is nude bodies in touch
strangers in longing
two people in love

My Lips

Oh! you miss out on much fun, instead of kneading
and pinching my breasts that are not aroused by your
rushed attention.
You should love my lips, wantonness at times are cravings
that need to be addressed. When I think of him or him,
not you, whom I share a bed?

You do not kiss my lips nor touch them passionately,
bright red, mocha, or creamy chocolate does not stir you.
Hello! Bottom Line is: You are not feeling me.

While my face is to the wall, I conjure up images of a
fairy tale man. I just as well put my headphones on and listen
to Maxwell while you are atop me doing your thing.
Oblivious that I have taken my tongue and raised it to the
tip of my lips and I begin to feel aroused. Ohhh!
I remember one of my lovers would place his finger to my lips
and I would suck as if drawing on a lollipop.

The call of water beckons me to play, ready are my lips between
my thighs. I slip the soap in and out of my vagina,
My vagina is so wet. I place my fingers there and then to my lips
to taste of me, to know who I am.
Lust overwhelms me, toys in place of my Man; who knows
not what pleasure my Lips bring to Him to ME.

I found a new toy, it was lying around.
By myself I am displaying some emotional attachment to
anything that resembles a head. From my man, I expect some
cuddling,
fondling, words of endearment.
I want him to know what my Pussy looks and smells like.
My new toy came as quite a surprise to me; I used it many times
when
I could not scratch the itch in the small of my back.

It is wood and has a base that forms five fingers.
Yet, at the handle it has wheels for massaging the body.
I roll it against my clitoris. Well! Hush! This is Liberation.
Keep on sleeping hubby with the cover pulled over your
head, continue to fall deaf to my needs and wants.
But, give me my wheels and if I can find a way to put some
Lips to these wheels, your ass will soon be out the door.

Calling Out to You

I call out to you
now that you are gone
the feeling of dread
has overwhelmed me
I seek a place to hide
a place made of warm flesh
with a heart that does not lie
to hurt
to feel again
what I felt with you
now that you are gone
I call out to you
in the fold of your limbs
I remembered I lied
length to length
our bodies entwined
our lips touch
so does our hearts
yet
there's always that ache
that tells me someday you shall part
in the eve of the night until the sun rises me
I watch you sleep
released from your mind,
all pressures of naught still you prefer to worry
over things as such
I've watched you still
I have watched you calm
All your faults maturing
when you are within my arms
It's only when you catch me
examining you closely
wondering if I know you too well
you disappear again into your world
now I too shall close just as a butterfly does
and hope when the wind blows it

carries my words only now that you are gone
I call out to you

The Wooden Board

I am suppose to know my duty
when you enter the bedroom
I am suppose to follow
there's no passion
there's no foreplay
there's no look of love
I am just here like this wooden board
that gives structure to this bed
into me you are banging
getting your satisfaction
selfish man
I saw your shadow on the wall
while you were pumping, pumping, pumping
and when I looked in another direction
towards the four winds
I left her there underneath you
while you were pumping, pumping, pumping

Letter Ode

In another woman's arms you slept
but in our bed our eyes rarely met
many nights I held myself and wept
I knew you had eyes for another
I will not go on being your quean
because this mop I sing to does not share
in hopes nor dreams
I long for the years past gone
maybe, because that is all I have left
what is the use of recollecting memories
and feeling sorry for myself
it is now and you I yearn but lost
I have lied here for so long lying to myself
it is time to think of divorce
it is going to be hard fighting down the years
but I will look towards tomorrow and my career
I will pack my bags and walk out the door
and attached to a Fifth of Bacardi shall be a
Letter Ode to You

My Solitude

My solitude is sometimes spent
lazing in the nude
and while the moon is peeping through
all my thoughts turn to you
pack away neatly are my fancy laces
and in my mind are the exotic places
and in my dreams are many faces and
every face is you

E

I noticed you
long before
and from my mind
I let you go
you think we met
at the grocery store
for you it is true
but I saw you long before
and from my mind I let
you go
I noticed you were always
alone
I was looking for the one
who you would place your
kiss upon
then…from my mind
I would let you go
time passes as time always does
you said hello to me outside of
the grocery store
how could you have known
we worked on different floors
until our eyes met in the
corridor
time passes as time always does
I noticed you long before
and from my mind I let you go

A Limn for You and I

This is a limn for you and I
because we could never be one another's
only love
I will release now all the sensuous moments
we have shared together
we have soul searched each other
in hope of unlocking the mystery hidden away
if only I could murmur sweet soft songs in
your ear and capture your essence in a crystal vase
I would savor it forever
if only I could assure you multiple orgasms every
time you are with me
over and over again

Men Can Not Write Me

Men cannot write me.
When read the inked lines inscribed,
realizations begin to form?
I am everything their minds imagine,
but my mirror does not reflect.

The fantasies they conjure are masked.
My skin is not white.
My breasts not erect.
My buttocks protrude outward.
Yet men paint me as round and firm.

Men write me in a childlike innocence.
Men write me as a little girl with thumb
in mouth, one leg behind and flowers in my hand.
Woman status is rarely reached, but when it arrives
I am dabbing a tear, finding a tie or starting a second rinse.

I am portrayed as inanimate. Men find me sexual when I
pout, cup my breasts, ride a 4 legged animal scantily clad or
lie with my legs spread.

Men cannot write me, how afraid of self they are. Their
fantasies are masked images which my mirror does not reflect.
Men write me, then denounce my independence.
Thus, when I choose to grow and explore my beauty is no more.

Been Such a Long Time

Been such a long time
been such a long time seeing you
I walked by the river today
I saw our images wavering on the waves
been such a long time seeing you
been such a long time

Drive Me Home

It feels good to sit down in my ride
and drive away
I love to run my hands along the sleek and
deep mounds of upholstery
every so often I will adjust the gear
side to side
back and forth
feels so good just driving
I am in control
I glimpse at the rear view mirror and I smile
the cushions on my ride are soft
Black and beautiful
such a fine body of exterior
I can slow down there is no rush
I must remember you are vulnerable
my ride has no choice but to let me take him
in the direction I choose to go
there is so much I can do with this stick shift
I lie back and feel the gear tilted
its so viable
with both my arms along his reclined seats
I begin to reach for the stick shift to Drive Me Home

Interchanged

She is I
with my face
and my body
I am her
with her face
And her body
look at us both
cross eyed
do you not see
she is me
I am her
and our vagina
Is ultimately the same too

Silly Love Poem

Time will you be mine
as the night shades the fading sun
and the stars come out to light the sky
as I sit with my head resting on my knees
I am writing lines that make no sense
a silly love poem

As I sit with my head resting on my knees
and a brisk air circles about my room
I think about our lovemaking to keep me warm
I just do not want to write a silly love poem

Now that you are out of my reach
should you ever stop by my way again
can you lend yourself for awhile
so that I may whisk away with you
and be able to throw away this silly love poem

I Will Think Bitch

You are such a degenerate.
If I sound cruel, stop and think these
are the same words you are saying to me.
Now! Why should I be your doormat.
As I lie here with my masturbatory dreams,
and you are with her foot loose and fancy free.

I am nothing jealous.
I am nothing if I can not love
I am nothing if I must sing to an empty room that
is filled with memories of you.

As I lie here caressing myself.
I look for my femininity that is slowly disappearing
from my body.
I am here being patient, waiting for you to come home
to our bed and your arms that lets me know you care.

I am just a fool.
I am nothing without fidelity at least to myself.
I am nothing without sincerity, I will give it my best.
And when all else fails, I will Think Bitch.

Beautiful Woman

Do not hide your eyes, when you cry?
Your tears are your mirrors, reflecting your soul.

Do not turn your face in shame, as you brush slightly
the dirt on the paned glass?

Do not close you mind altogether?
Everything shall get better in time.

As you stand there brushing slightly the dirt on
the paned glass.